The SCHOOL FOR CATS

The SCHOOL
FOR CATS

Story and Pictures by
ESTHER AVERILL

THE NEW YORK REVIEW CHILDREN'S COLLECTION
New York

THIS IS A NEW YORK REVIEW BOOK
PUBLISHED BY THE NEW YORK REVIEW OF BOOKS
435 Hudson Street, New York, NY 10014
www.nyrb.com

Published in the United States of America

Library of Congress Catalog-in-Publication Data
Averill, Esther Holden.
The school for cats / by Esther Averill.
p. cm.— (New York Review children's collection)
"A Jenny's Cat Club book."
Summary: Captain Tinker sends Jenny Linsky off to boarding school for the summer,
but when another student frightens her, she tries to run away.
ISBN 1-59017-173-X (alk. paper)
[1. Cats—Fiction. 2. Boarding schools—Fiction. 3. Schools—Fiction.]
I. Title. II. Series.
PZ7.A935Sch 2005
[E]—dc22
2005008880

ISBN-13: 978-1-59017-173-8

Cover design by Louise Fili Ltd

Printed in the United States of America on acid-free paper
9 10 8

J. Linsky

MANNERS
100%

COOPERATION
98%

FOR

L. J. C.

Once upon a time there was a Boarding School for Cats off in the country, in a white house surrounded by a field of daisies. Cats and kittens, mostly from the towns and cities, went there. Sometimes they went because their masters were obliged to go away from home on trips or business. Sometimes a cat was sent to School to learn good manners.

3

One of the cats was Pickles. He was a big, spotted cat who lived in the winter in New York City with the firemen in the Engine House. But in the summer, when the streets were hot, the firemen sent Pickles to Boarding School to get the country air and to improve his manners.

The firemen let Pickles take his own Hook and Ladder which they had built for him. And as he was a special Fire Department cat, the Teacher gave him the privilege of having it at School. He loved to drive this Hook and Ladder through the fields of daisies. Best of all, he liked to chase the little cats with it.

One day in June, a little black cat went to School on board the train from New York City. She was supposed to stay at School while her master was away at sea.

Her name was Jenny Linsky and she traveled on the train all by herself, inside a wicker basket. Now and then the Train Conductor spoke to her.

"Cheer up. School can be fun," he said.

Jenny did not believe him. She had never been to any School and she was scared.

The Teacher met Jenny at the country station and drove her down a bumpy road to School. By the time they reached School, Jenny was so frightened that she crawled beneath the parlor sofa. The understanding Teacher let her eat supper there, alone.

After supper, when the pupils trooped

into the parlor for the Evening Lesson in Manners, Jenny watched them from beneath the sofa.

Pickles entered on his Hook and Ladder and after he had parked it carefully behind the radio, the Teacher said, "Now that we are ready, let us sing our little song."

The pupils sang:

> "If you will learn Manners,"
> The dear Teacher said,
> "Then you shall have Catnip
> Before going to bed."
>
> "Oh, give us our Catnip,"
> The kittens insisted.
> "Without any Catnip
> Our Manners get twisted."
>
> "Untwist your best Manners,"
> The kind Teacher said,
> "For you shall have Catnip
> Before going to bed."

"Honk! Honk!" said Pickles when the song was over.

Then the Teacher took a jar of catnip from the parlor shelf.

"Will the cats and kittens form a line?" she said.

They formed a line, beginning with the smallest cat and ending with big Pickles.

The cat in front stood up,

dipped his paw into the jar of catnip, took a pawful of the tasty leaves and stepped aside. The next cat did as the first had done, and so did all the others, each in turn.

"Oh, aren't they clever!" Jenny thought. "I could never learn to do what they are doing."

Afterward, the pupils put their catnip on the floor and sniffed and rolled in it until the clock struck nine and it was bedtime. Then they scampered into the big bedroom and got on their little beds like angels.

These beds had mattresses and pillows, and the posts were made of logs so that the pupils could sharpen their claws before breakfast.

Jenny was carried by the Teacher to a bed which had a bright red scarf on it.

"This is your own bed," the Teacher said

to Jenny. "Sleep well, and in the morning you can get acquainted with your schoolmates."

Jenny lay down and tucked her little black nose in the scarf she had worn to School. It was the scarf her dear master, Captain Tinker, had knitted for her with his own hands. It made her very homesick.

After the Teacher went away, one of the cats asked Jenny if she would like to join in a pillow fight. Jenny was too homesick to reply.

Meanwhile the Fire Cat, Pickles, had gone to the closet and taken out his fire truck. He sat down on the driver's seat, honked the horn and cried, "Make way for the Hook and Ladder!"

Then he drove toward Jenny's bed and bumped it. Jenny was so startled that she leaped and landed on the floor. Big Pickles chased her.

A cat called out, "Go easy, Pickles!"

But Pickles drove as fast as he could drive.

And Jenny ran as fast
as she could run.

At last she saw a fireplace and she crawled
beneath a chair to get there. Big Pickles fol-
lowed her and collided with the chair. It fell
over with a *bang!*

The Teacher had been downstairs, sewing
in the parlor. When she heard the rumpus,

she rushed up to find out what was happening.

She reached the bedroom just in time to see a black hind leg and tail disappearing up the chimney. Pickles was sitting on his Hook and Ladder, looking very innocent. The other cats were lying quietly on their beds. But the Teacher knew exactly what had happened.

She turned to Pickles and said, "Naughty Pickles, you have driven Jenny up the chimney."

There was great excitement in the School next morning. The new pupil, Jenny Linsky, was still up the chimney.

Pickles shouted, "I've got a Hook and Ladder! I can get her down!"

Some laughed at this, but others thought that Pickles had already been too rough with little Jenny.

Everybody thought that Jenny would come down for breakfast. She did not. So after breakfast, when the Teacher shooed the cats outdoors, they climbed the apple trees behind the School and tried to look down the chimney.

Jenny was way up the chimney. She had climbed as far as pos- sible—and as she sat there on a narrow brick, she said stubbornly to herself, "I won't eat, I won't answer anyone. I'll just stay here."

So when the Teacher poked her head up

the chimney and called, "Jenny! Jenny Linsky!"—there was no answer.

And later, when the Teacher called again to Jenny, there was silence in the chimney.

But suddenly there was a sneeze.

A piece of soot had got inside of Jenny's nose and when she sneezed, the brick that she was sitting on broke loose. A heap of soot poured down the chimney, and in the middle of the soot, right on the floor, sat Jenny Linsky.

The Teacher stooped to pick her up. Jenny squirmed, leaped through an open window, and ran down the road as fast as possible. She ran so fast, in fact, that there was not a speck of soot left on her when, toward noon, she reached the Village. Here she found a place of safety on the front pew of an empty church.

Not long afterward, while she was still inside the church, Jenny caught a whiff of School, and then the sound of voices. One voice was the Teacher's; the other, a boy's.

The boy said, "No, I haven't seen a black cat anywhere. What happened? Did they fight?"

"Not exactly," said the Teacher. "It was Jenny's first night at School, at any school. A bigger cat, named Pickles, scared her with his Hook and Ladder. She ran off. I've hunted everywhere and cannot find her."

"Lady," the boy said, "is it true that you teach Reading and Arithmetic to cats?"

"No," replied the Teacher. "Cats use a different kind of knowledge. I only try to teach them Manners and Cooperation, which means courtesy and getting on with one another."

Jenny, by this time, had crawled through an open, stained glass window.

She hurried to the railroad tracks and sniffed the air . . . and although New York City was a hundred miles away, she caught its smell.

"Home is the place for me," she said, and turned in that direction.

As she walked alongside the tracks, through fields of daisies, she said, "You can have the daisies. Give *me* the sidewalks of New York."

She rather liked the sound of this. So she repeated it and wished that Pickles might have been near-by to hear her say it.

As she approached the station, a train came roaring up the tracks. Jenny scrambled

18

to the station roof, in time to see the train stop right below her. It was the train from New York City, the very train on which she herself had traveled the day before.

On the train steps stood the Train Conductor with two covered baskets in his hand. And when the Teacher hurried to the platform, Jenny held her breath.

The Train Conductor gave the baskets to the Teacher, saying, "Here are two new pupils: Florio and Tiger James. They're quite a lively pair."

"I know them well," replied the Teacher. "They've been to School before. But oh, Conductor! the little black cat that you brought yesterday has run away!"

"Not Captain Tinker's cat!" exclaimed the Train Conductor. "Dear me, the Captain will be very worried."

Then the train, with a warning toot, started up the tracks while Jenny, on the roof, began to feel ashamed of having run away. Besides, the two new cats were the most attractive cats she had ever seen, though she could only see their faces at the windows of the baskets.

One cat was golden-colored and his name was Florio. He seemed so beautiful and kind that Jenny's little heart went pit-a-pat. She would have been glad to follow Florio to the end of the wide, wide world. She hung on every word he said.

He said to his companion, who was a striped cat named Tiger James, "Oh, Tiger, didn't we have fun at School last summer when we chased the Rooster?"

"We sure did," chuckled Tiger James. "And do you remember how we used to swap beds?"

"And all the lovely pillow fights!" laughed Florio.

"And all the pillows that burst!" laughed Tiger James.

"Oh," thought Jenny. "School must be fun when Florio and Tiger James are there."

Then Florio said to Tiger James, "I wonder what new cats will be at School this summer."

"I hope there's some regular fellows," said Tiger James. "I'm looking forward to lots of good times."

At this point, the Teacher put the two gay students into the School car, and as they drove down the country road, poor little Jenny wished with all her heart that she were going with them.

"I'd love to see a pillow fight," she sighed. "I'd love to climb the apple trees and chase the Rooster."

The more she thought, the more she reasoned with herself this way: "Captain Tinker wanted me to go to School. He'll be very disappointed in me if I run away. I ought to go back. I *will* go back and I'll just say to Pickles . . . I'll say . . ."

Jenny did not know what she would say to the big, spotted creature, Pickles, who had chased her with his Hook and Ladder, frightened her and made her run away from School. He was too big to fight with her paws, but she knew she must do something.

"I must not let him tease me," Jenny told herself. "I must make Pickles understand that I am I. But how to do it? I shall think about it on my way to School."

23

She climbed carefully down the vine behind the station and began to follow the
traces of the School car in the dusty road.
Probably she would have soon reached
School if a motorcycle had not sped up the
road.

Jenny thought that somebody was trying
to catch her. If she were caught, how could
she explain that she belonged at School? It
would be better to take no chances.

She leaped from the road and tore across
the daisy fields as fast as her black legs would
carry her. She did not stop until she reached
the forest.

"I'll hide here," she decided.

J enny had never been in a forest, but strangely enough she was not frightened. The odd smells oozing from the earth and trees delighted her. The farther she went, the more the forest seemed like something that had happened to her long ago.

Night was falling, and the cats at School would soon be on their little beds.

"Won't they be surprised when I get back and tell them that I've seen a forest," Jenny thought. "Won't Pickles be surprised! Perhaps I ought to take some small things with me—just to show where I've been."

So she went on and on, looking for a wee

25

flower, a small bird's feather and a pretty berry when suddenly, ahead of her, she saw the bushy tail of a tremendous Fox!

Jenny shivered and dashed up a tree. But the old, wicked Fox had heard her.

"Yap," snarled the Fox. "Yap. Yap."

But when he turned to find her, she had climbed so high among the leaves and branches that he could not see her. Nor could he understand what kind of beast she was.

This Fox knew all the forest animals. He could tell them by their smells. But the smells which drifted through the air from

Jenny's fur were smells he did not know. They were the smells of Boarding School and trains and New York City. The Fox became so muddled that after a while he went scowling to his den.

Then Jenny climbed to earth so quietly that nobody but the birds could hear her. And by running quickly she got safely through the forest. The morning sun was rising as she skipped across the daisy fields. No one saw her as she hurried down the road.

She reached School in time for breakfast with the other pupils. To her joy, her place in the breakfast row was between the two new cats, Florio and Tiger James, whom she had seen when she was hiding at the station.

Down the row was Pickles.

In his own queer way, Pickles was as glad

as anyone to have the little lost cat back. But all that he could think of was to run into the parlor and bring out his Hook and Ladder. When he reached the breakfast room, he paused in the doorway, leaned his elbow on the steering wheel and gazed at Jenny.

"Oh dear," thought Jenny. "He's going to try again to drive me away from School. He's going to make me lose my fun."

But Florio whispered to her, "Show him who you are. We'll help you if you need us."

Tiger James said, "We're your friends."

These two new friends gave Jenny courage and when Pickles honked his horn at her, she bared her claws.

Then Pickles, looking straight at Jenny, shouted, "MAKE WAY FOR THE HOOK AND LADDER!"

Jenny, looking straight at Pickles,

shouted, "MAKE WAY FOR THE BIG-
GEST FIRE ON EARTH!"

She flew at him so madly that you could
see fire spurting from her ears. Big Pickles
ducked and Jenny struck the ladders. The
truck toppled over, with Pickles beneath it.

He crawled out finally and rising slowly to his feet, gazed in admiration at the little black cat who had upset his Hook and Ladder.

After a moment he held out his paw and said to her, "You win."

Never again did Pickles chase Jenny with his Hook and Ladder.

Never again did he tease any little cat. He saved his rough tricks for the cats as big as he was. As for the littler cats, he tried not to tease them but to please them. This was the beginning of his education.

This was also the beginning of one of the happiest summers Jenny ever had. She shared in all the good times of her schoolmates, climbed the apple trees and went on picnics.

On the closing day of School, when the pupils were getting ready to go home,

Pickles, who was returning to the Fire Department, said to Jenny, "Jenny, why don't you visit me some time? You'd like the firemen and I could take you on a real, true Hook and Ladder to a real, true fire."

"Oh, Pickles," Jenny cried, "I'd love to!"

A warm glow filled her heart because she realized that the friendships she had made at School would last forever.

ESTHER AVERILL (1902–1992) began her career as a storyteller drawing cartoons for her local newspaper. After graduating from Vassar College in 1923, she moved first to New York City and then to Paris, where she founded her own publishing company. The Domino Press introduced American readers to artists from all over the world, including Feodor Rojankovsky, who later won a Caldecott Award.

In 1941, Averill returned to the United States and found a job in the New York Public Library while continuing her work as a publisher. She wrote her first book about the red-scarfed, mild-mannered cat Jenny Linsky in 1944, modeling its heroine on her own shy cat. Averill would eventually write twelve more tales about Miss Linsky and her friends (including the I Can Read Book *The Fire Cat*), each of which was eagerly awaited by children all over the United States (and their parents, too).